An Anthology

# Seven Degrees Off Horror

## Daniel Nick

# Contents

# Introduction

Collected in these pages are seven of my stories that I'd label "Horror". But I'm an odd duck and I tend to view the world a tad bit differently than many others. Some people might argue a few stories here have no business being in a Horror anthology, and maybe they'd be right...assuming they were in charge of this book.

They are not.

I see Horror differently than some. Without getting too deeply into it, I've seen real horror. I've never been on a battlefield, I've never met a monster, I've never run into horror that breaks the minds of humanity. But you know what? Yes I have. There's more than one type of battlefield, monsters often live in the bedroom next to the victims, and I've cried myself to sleep more than once having spent my career trying to mend their broken minds. I know real horror, and it doesn't need a full moon to come out, a scary decrepit mansion to reside in, or to drink blood to live.

Yes, there is a fun Vampire short story, and a haunted house. There is some nastiness and some gruesome death contained in these pages, for sure. I've found that when I'm just writing to hone my craft or to throw down ideas, they're almost always what I would consider horror (no, I'm not going to psychoanalyze myself here, I promise).

Then again, there is a story here that conveys the horror of what humans do to each other, but nobody so much as gets a nosebleed.

I tried to lay out the anthology so that the stories go from "Traditional Monster" and grow progressively less so. So you traditionalists get a fun short Vampire story right away and a Werewolf flash fic. Maybe, if you like it, you'll stick around for the haunted house, the nightmare, the teacher's last day at work, the students' big test, and the Hookers from Outer Space.

I hope you enjoy the stories, and I hope you can see past the words on the page to the heart of the matter. I promise - each one of these stories has elements of the horrific, and each and every one lives on my computer in the "Horror Short Story" folder.

Even the Hookers from Outer Space.

This one goes out to all the people who appear as characters in these stories.

I'm sorry, but you did something to earn it. Probably something like supported me when I was down, or joining me as we fought to provide a real life for kids who otherwise would have been denied them.

Hell, maybe you just had the poor taste to become part of my family.

So there's that...

# Little Gods

## A vampire tale

"**W**ho the fuck is this dead guy on my bed?"

Shit, I was just getting to like this town.

O.K., here's the situation; I'm something of a deep sleeper, but I've got few defenses to protect myself from would be saviors of the world. One of these is an ability to kill in my sleep. I need this instinctual protection, you see, because I'm the bad guy. You would call me Evil with the capital "E".

Can't blame you really, after all you're just food to me. I'm the beast, the hunter, and the spouter of bad clichés. But, for the most part, I prefer to work in anonymity. So when I wake up holding a dead man by his crushed throat, I always look for a large hammer and pathetic little wooden stake on the ground. If – like now – I find them, it kind of rules out random burglary. Your kind have found me and know that I am a Vampire.

Tossing the body off to the side, I survey my bedroom. Tasteful yet understated. Except for the dead guy.

The corpse obviously thrashed about in his death throes; the room is a wreck. The wall near my headboard has holes where the dying man kicked and flopped into it. An expensive antique lamp and the blonde

Heywood-Wakefield nightstand have been destroyed. It lies on its side next to my custom made, sled-style king bed. Figures. I had the bed built to match the nightstand.

The fabulously expensive handmade Persian rug is twisted up in the dead man's feet, and judging from the foul odor in the room, the corpse lost control of his bowels when he died.

I look closer. Sure enough, the carpet is soaked. Ruined by a dead man's piss.

The only question now is how many others are there? They never come alone, and they never have the balls to stay and finish the job after my sleeping form kills the first one to approach. I mean, be honest, would you hang around after your fearless leader was killed by a fiend who didn't even bother to wake up to do it?

But this one is still very warm, so his cohorts must be nearby. Also it is dark now, they are on my turf. I will find every one of them and make sure they are all dead, but first I need sustenance, and like I said, this one's still warm. Breakfast in bed.

The blood is no longer flowing so the traditional neck bite is out, but that's O.K. We vampires don't wear tuxedos and capes, but we can do a few really cool tricks. We are so much more than you know. We are Gods.

I will my body to shift from its human form, and a six-foot, attractive man (attractive? I'm fucking gorgeous) with flowing brown hair and a wiry, athletic body transforms into your worst nightmares. My body thickens and hunches as if my spine can't hold the sudden increase in weight. A groan escapes from my throat as my forehead takes on a sickening slant back to my receding hairline, and my jaws sprout a mouthful of razor sharp teeth. My fingers elongate and the nails on them harden, and I look out on the world with glowing red eyes. Then with a strength you humans wouldn't believe until I used it on you, I rip the heart out of his chest and swallow it whole.

Don't let bad fiction fool you, blood may make the world go round, but my kind can eat anything. I prefer souls.

Once breakfast is over, I squat next to the ruined Persian rug and focus my thoughts outward. I allow my mind to be open and receptive to the emotions of the living creatures around me. This part of the hunt always scares me. See, I don't know exactly what it is I'm doing, but for my kind it's an instinctual part of what I call our "predatory package".

Yup. Vampires are empaths. It works most of the time without any serious side effects. Most of the time.

Sometimes it can come back on me with such force that I'll sit en-raptured for the entire night bathed in an intoxicating symphony of loves, hates, fears, and passions, completely oblivious to the physical world around me.

Anyway, this time there is no backlash and I can handle the influx of feelings. Even though I dread this particular endeavor, its practice pays off and I feel an ungodly amount of terror that, experience shows, only a monster like me can inspire. It is barely two miles away, which is not at all surprising because these idiots always park the car way out in the boonies in order to better their chances of sneaking up on what is, lets face it, effectively a comatose villain.

For some reason they never think about the potential need for a speedy escape. Research people, research! You could come in here with the Notre Dame Marching Band playing and if it ain't dark, I ain't waking! Of course that doesn't mean that I am defenseless. You could ask the poor shmuck at my feet about that except he ain't talking.

Back to the amateurs here. There has to be no more than four, maybe five people in the one vehicle racing away from me. With the amount of psycho babble coming from their minds it's hard to tell the exact number but, what the fuck, empathic mental probing is not an exact science now is it?

I can tell that the driver is so scared that he can hardly control the big...van! Yes, he is driving a van and he is crying and can't see where he's going. I'd better get to him before he crashes the damn machine into a tree and kills them all. That's my job.

I don't bother to revert back to my human guise. Even so, they're about six miles away by the time I hide the damage to the outside of my brand new house and get started after them. It will take me about four or five minutes to catch up if they don't crash first, but that's the chance I have to take.

So I start out after them at a swift, albeit supernatural, pace. I'm not using anything more than my enhanced strength and endurance to chase them down, but that still puts me in the same class as your average sports cars. And I can go off road.

This all sounds impossible, but for Vampires it is just second nature, we've been doing this stuff since before the birth of science. Long before Aristotle, Socrates, and Plato (or, the three stooges as I like to call them) fucked up the world far worse than my kind ever dreamed of by giving birth to the scientific thought process, Greeks, Phoenicians, Egyptians, Chinese, and virtually anywhere nomads came to trade news, we were there. We were in their stories, we were in their nightmares, we were in their midst. So while logic and knowledge have grown to rule men's minds, there has always been this second nature people have had to deal with.

Actually though, all this nature talk is unfair to humans, because it's more than just nature. No matter what anyone may say, when it comes to my kind, science and nature take a back seat to the supernatural. Sorry, I know that it's not currently popular to think this way, but the sad fact remains that our origins are not of this level of existence. There is a God, just not the ones my victims pray to for deliverance, and and there is a Devil.

There always has and always will be a struggle between chaos and order, empathy and sociopathy, "right" and "wrong" and there are armies on both sides. Humans are bit players, pawns; and like pawns have little real power on the chessboard other than sheer numbers. I don't know what piece I am, but I feel pretty sure it ain't the bishop.

Up ahead I see the van lurching and weaving from side to side, but not nearly as bad as expected. That's a shame because it means that they are collecting their wits and calming down.

Too bad for them because it will make their death that much more cruel. To have that false hope that you made it away safely only to have my hurtling form tear through the side of your van and kill everyone in it, well, it chokes me up just thinking about it.

The tall one sitting against the side I come through dies instantly, his spinal cord severed, body ripped nearly in half. In the gore spattered interior I have time to notice the raw terror in the eyes of the tubby one with the bad pockmarked face before I slam his head into the window and then fling him all the way to the back of the van like a rag doll. That leaves only two left both still strapped in to their seat belts up front. Neither one has had time to move yet, but the dawning comprehension in their eyes tells me that they know they are already dead.

Something's wrong here, and I pause for a fraction of an instant before yanking the passenger out of his seat and tearing a good portion of his neck out to spray his fresh blood down my throat. The driver has lost his mind and motor functions and the van is slowing down of its own accord, but not fast enough. The road turns and the van, unguided, does not. We tear through the guardrail at about forty miles an hour and, of course, crash into a tree. No surprise, I go airborne through the front windshield and hit the dirt, my body digging an impressive furrow through the soil.

That hurt, and while I lay there recovering, I try to take stock of exactly what is going on here. Something was wrong with that whole scene inside the van, something false about it all. None of them had a weapon in their hand-- none were prepared. Hell, none of them even seemed to be in that great of shape.

That's what it is! These kids are not only amateurs; they don't even know what game they're playing! When a group of humans discover who and what I am, they are usually much more organized in their attempt to assassinate me. At least before I wake. Then it is always the same, screaming and crying, blood and carnage.

You do not, I repeat, *do not* go into combat against me or mine without some serious muscle and firepower. Christ, I think I saw a baseball bat sharpened to a point in there!

"Like there is a fucking chance in hell of somebody sticking me with that!" I yell out loud to nobody.

Okay. I think it's time to smack these puny humans around until they realize how ridiculous it is to play at being Van Helsing when they should be playing Rambo. It's the modern age, people! Bring guns for fucks sake!

I get up and stagger to the smoking van. Flames are beginning to lick at the dark blue Ford's undercarriage, and two occupants still have beating hearts. A god just knows these things.

After pulling the two still-living kids a few yards away from the vehicle fire, I drop them at the base of a tree and look them over. The driver is a big man, looks like a football player, and so is obviously the leader of this little outing. He's got the looks of one used to telling others what to do.

I shall call the other one Pimple-face. He's the tubby one I threw around earlier. He's got a gash on his scalp from having his head run through glass, and it is bleeding copiously. Smells delicious. He also has a machete strapped onto his belt that I didn't notice earlier. Lucky kid or he'd have been dead in the van.

Kneeling down, I wake the boys with a couple of rough slaps.

Laughing, I ask, "Are we having fun yet? Wake up! Time for school, kids!"

Mister Athlete just stares at nothing, drooling. He's done. Pimple-face, on the other hand, leans against the tree and glances down at his toy knife. To disabuse the punk of any thoughts of heroism, I decide to set the record straight.

Turning my back on athlete-as-coma-boy, I say, "Nice knife. Let's you and I get one thing perfectly clear, any mortal who has ever fought a Vampire and lived to tell of it and – embarrassingly enough, there are a few – will say the same thing; forget it. Forget everything you have ever heard, read, watched, or in any other way been informed about Vampires. In reality, the only sure way to kill a Vampire is to find another Vampire who will do it for you. One of them will die. Hopefully, the one you wanted."

I lean in close toward Pimple-face and say, "I'm talking to you boy, you had best answer me."

"S-So what about those humans that have fought and lived?" he stuttered.

An actual question? Well. I wasn't expecting that. Usually, this is the point that they start begging for mercy. Obviously, this kid is in denial. He simply cannot accept that he has less than five minutes left on this earth. Still, might as well answer the child. How often does an opportunity to explain to humans the difference between gods and men come along?

"Well, I suppose that they have survived through a rare combination of luck and ego. They had the luck, and we have one hell of an ego." I smiled and started to warm up to the little talk.

"To explain what I mean I have to back up to the whole "forget about it all" thing. You see, wooden stakes through the heart do not kill us, not even when it's a cute blond or a learned doctor doing it."

"How can that be? All the literature, the legends..." he trailed off.

"Historically, wooden stakes were part of a three-part chore for you would-be slayers of evil. The actual ritual was as follows: the stake, the sword, and the fire.

"Why?"

"Why? Well, that's simple. The stake was used to pin our bodies in place long enough to behead us with a stout sword. Let me stress here that this attack is used on SLEEPING Vampires, not ones that are awake and pissed. No one would ever be able to stake an awake Vampire."

Waving off the ludicrous thought, I continued, "Anyway, cutting our heads off can indeed kill us. We are living beings after a fashion, and without a brain, and with our blood on the floor instead of in our bodies, we die. Then of course you had to burn our bodies till there was nothing left in order to prevent a supposed contamination of the town."

"Supposed?"

"Supposed. We are not a pestilence spread throughout the world turning all we touch into demon spawn. If that were true, everyone you know would be a Vampire right now. I have fed upon thousands of bodies. Thousands, boy! And I happen to know that there are considerably less than five hundred Vampires in all the world."

I stood up and stretched out a bit before kneeling back down to continue. "You have to give weight to the times. They didn't know any better back in prehistory, so better safe than sorry. They tended to burn anything they didn't trust back in those days, but even then, they knew the place of the stake in the scheme of things. It was only supposed to occupy the Vampire's mind long enough for the real weapon to remove said mind from the body attached to it.

"Thousands?" he whispered, shrinking against the tree as if to disappear into it.

Ignoring him, I continued, "Now sometimes they didn't wait for the beheading and went right to the fire. That wasn't so successful because wood burns faster than we do, and I don't care how painful a stake in your chest is, fire hurts worse, so as soon as the stake was weakened from the flames a Vampire would break free."

"Our only flaw, if we have one, is that we are too powerful. In the night we are virtually invincible. We are Gods. It's easy to forget that if the head leaves the body, we're just as dead as last night's dinner. Hubris. Vanity. The downfall of the Morning Star himself, Archangel Lucifer. I've never met him, but if he exists, you can bet your ass that he thinks pretty highly of himself."

I straighten up and say, "Christ, I haven't made a speech like that in ages. Felt good."

Suddenly, the fat boy relaxes and says, "Virtually invincible? Thanks for all the information, I'll remember it."

"For about five more seconds anyway." I lean in towards the sitting snack and begin to transform back into my true form for feeding, teeth sprouting like sickles and dripping blood.□

With a Herculean effort, Pimple-face forces himself to smile right back, fingers the machete, and says; "I don't think so, Demon."

"Vampire," I say, frowning. This isn't going right at all.

"Whatever. You don't know as much as you think."

"Whatever? I'll show you whatever!" I rise up to my full height; fangs extended, and claws flexed; as terrifying a sight as likely to be seen on this earth.

Pimple-face nods and yells, "Now!"

Then from behind him, I hear a line from a B-grade movie, "Die, hellspawn! Die!"

Furious, I turn around just in time to see the formerly comatose driver, silhouetted in roaring flames, ram a sharpened baseball bat under my sternum, through my heart, and out my back, pinning me to the tree.

Pimple-face, the real leader, stands and swings his machete with two hands.

Aww fu—

# Pack Leader

## Werewolf Flash fiction

"**N**o shit, there I was," he said again, "surrounded by ten of the meanest werewolves you'd ever hate to see, and me with only nine shots in my pistol. I tell ya, I almost lost my cool, but..."

"But since this story's just bullshit, you managed to live to inflict your lies on us."

Old Jake looked over at the young man who had interrupted him and growled under his breath. This confrontation had been building all night and Jake was looking forward to killing the little punk.

"Well, old man," the youngster named Petyr, said, "am I right? Did you kill all the big bad werewolves?"

"Don't tell me that werewolves can't travel in packs Petyr."

"Oh I suppose they might, but I've never seen more than one at a time." He turned to the other hunters sitting around the fireplace, "Have any of you ever seen a Werewolf Pack?"

Surprisingly to both Petyr and Jake, one arm went up. There was no hand attached.

It got really quiet, really fast.

Johann Koenig–the amputee–never said anything unless it was impor-tant. There wasn't a more respected man in our line of work. We all knew he was the best hunter ever; at least before he had lost his hand. We waited in silence for him to speak.

"Many years ago," he began, "I was hunting one of the Longcoats up in the Urals – your country, Petyr – and I saw many tracks converge in the forest. At first, I thought it was just a pack of regular wolves, and planned to move on, when out of the corner of my eye I saw a human footprint. Not a boot print mind you, but a naked footprint. No sooner had I realized what that meant, than I met...Him. He walked out naked and shivering, but he had a smile on his face that let me know he was confident and unafraid. I dared not lift my gun."

Johann looked around as he stood and thoughtfully rubbed the stump of his left arm on the barrel of his shotgun. He broke open the breach and checked the twelve-gauge cartridge holding a silver slug as if assuring himself that it was there.

Walking to the two arguing hunters, he continued. "We wound up talking for a long time, that werewolf and I. He knew that I could kill him where he stood, and I knew that if I did, his pack would tear me apart. It took a long time until we," Johan shrugged with a wry mirth, "understood each other well enough to slowly go our separate ways. He didn't exactly tell me his life story, but I learned much."

He stood inches away from Petyr's face and said, "I found out many things about werewolves you lot don't know, such as they don't think much about us hunters."

He looked the young man up and down, "Their attitudes are a lot like yours, Petyr. Brash and arrogant. I also found out -assuming he didn't lie to me- that we've had it backwards all along. The wolf is their real form, and that they can appear as any human they wish."

His eyes never leaving Petyr's, he leveled his shotgun at Jake as he said, "But do you know what I remember best about that talk?"

Petyr shook his head mutely.

"He started each story with 'No shit, there I was'."

And everybody looked over at Old Jake.

# Born of Pain

## A twist on the Haunted House

Jerry knelt in front of the bedroom door sweating. The sour smell of uncertainty and intense fear surrounded him and the rest of his SWAT team. Nothing was different about this particular job – officially. It was supposed to be a routine sweep and clear. Jerry and the guys had done this dozens of times in the past. It should have been a piece of cake for this team because after all, they were the best of the best. New York City Fucking SWAT. Yet not a single one of them wanted to be here, and most were starting to think that they would never be leaving.

Big Dan, Jerry's second in command, looked at his watch.

"What time is it now Big D?" asked Frankie, giggling that manic little laugh he developed about halfway through this nightmare.

"It's about three goddamn seconds since the last time I looked." he snarled back.

Jerry stopped the argument before it got started by saying, "Lighten up you two. We're on the same team here. It's been three seconds, and that's that."

And that, in a nutshell, was the main problem. Big Dan had intentionally not looked at his watch for at least two hours, yet time had only moved along about three fucking seconds. It wasn't his watch's fault. If any of the others were to check their chronographs, it would have read the same thing--three measly ticks. According to their watches, they had been in this pit of hell for fifty-nine seconds, but according to their bodies, they had been here for somewhere around two days. Two days of darkness and fear.

This wasn't some hallucination like Darren had thought. They all had thick stubble on their faces and stomachs that never stopped growling. All of them were suffering from mild cases of sleep deprivation, and most importantly, they were all seeing the same things. Still, that hadn't stopped Darren and Mitch from taking off to search for their own escape. The part that really sucked was that there was nothing Jerry could have done to stop them; short of shooting them both, and that wasn't going to happen. These guys had been through too much shit together for that to ever go down. Hell, Mitch had a wife, Evelyn, and a cute little girl named Samantha. Darren also just happened to be little Sam's Godfather! So in the end, they had run off and disappeared unmolested.

The first rule in an unusual or unforeseen situation was to stick together. Now instead of five well-armed, ass-kicking police officers, there were only three scared men. There had been no radio contact with either Mitch or Darren since they left well over fourteen hours ago (nineteen seconds).

To top it all, this strange passage of time wasn't the only thing contributing to the officers' world-class mind fuck. The other bite in the ass was that this relatively small crackhouse had, at last count, three hundred and fifty-seven rooms. Could there be a more unusual situation than this? Jerry thought fucking not.

As the men prepared for the assault, Jerry tested his night vision equipment and thought back one last time to the start of this mess.

□The men were on a tight time schedule. From the moment of entry, they had exactly one minute to secure the first floor and tie off the rooms. Tying off rooms simply meant that after they cleared a room and secured it, they would string a line across the doorway to indicate that there were no perps hiding out there.

After securing the bottom floor, they would head up to the second story, and repeat the process. But this time they would have the rooftop snipers and spotters keeping an eye on them through the windows and calling in with any info they might have on the whereabouts of hiding junkies.

When they had stormed over the threshold of the drug den the guys had fanned out covering each other in a calm professional way bred from years of training. They had faith in each other and in themselves. They were used to working with the best, and this night's mission was textbook, right?

Wrong.

First off, the raid was set for twenty-one hundred hours, but about an hour before that, right after dark, they had seen the Big Man himself, Chauncy Winegrate stroll in the front door with his muscle right behind him. He was the reason that SWAT was here tonight. Undercover had been on this Dope peddler for months, and word had finally come to them about his planned appearance tonight at this house of death. About thirty minutes later, a rooftop spotter reported that Chauncey had just drawn his pistol and shot an addict for an unknown reason. Brass was ecstatic! A police officer had just witnessed a murder. Chauncey Winegrate was going down, no doubt about it.

Then, just before the order to go, a bright flash of light lit the interior of the building for about three seconds. This caused a panic back at the command. There wasn't supposed to be any source of power to this building. Did Chauncy and his goons bring in a generator or something? This could screw up the whole works and negate SWAT's nighttime advantage. But eventually, the powers that be decided that it couldn't have been a genera-tor because the light hadn't stayed on, so the operation was green-lighted. The SWAT team went through about twenty minutes late because of the brass.

Surveillance crews had been watching junkies come in and out of the place all night, but upon entry, the team found nobody: no junkies, no muscle, no Chauncy. Caught up in the danger of the moment, they failed to realize that they were rushing through more rooms than a house this size had any right to have. Finally, Jerry realized that the inside was too big and took charge of his group.

"All right everyone," Jerry called out "backtrack, stay in visual of each other, and someone tell me what the fuck's going on here. Anyone?"

Big Dan just shrugged and said, "They didn't cover this in the briefing, sir."

No one laughed.

Suddenly, Frankie yelled out "Sir!  The rooftop spotters; they should have seen anyone exiting the back."

Swearing, Jerry called out on his voice-activated mic, "Unit two, this is unit one, what do you see?  Repeat: Has anybody left the back of the building?  Do you copy?"

"Dan, call the rooftop. I'm not getting anything."

"Unit two, check in."

No one answered despite repeated efforts by all the team members. No talking, no response; just preternatural quiet. Mitch looked at his watch.

"Uh, sir?  My watch stopped."  Instinctually, everyone else looked down at his own timepiece. That's when things went from strange to stranger.

"Mine too," said Darren.

"Hey--Big D, how many rooms you think we just went through?"

"I counted thirteen," said Frankie

"Too damn many." interrupted Jerry. "Let's go back to the front door and get out of here.

"Uh...O.K. sir. Which way?"

"Shit. Well then, let's start tying off the doors and use a little logic to get out of this mess. We'll find the exit out of here soon enough. Everybody stow your night vision. Flashlights will do until we find some bad guys."

They were lost inside a small, two-story townhouse, their only light coming from the occasional burning candle left by a junkie and each other's flashlights. Over the next several hours, many theories and explanations would be put forward by the guys as to why they couldn't find the friggin' front door, most of which were quickly discarded. They passed through dingy room after dingy room--always tying off the doorway after they passed through--surrounded by nothing but the oppressive sights and smells of rot and decay. They stayed by each other not out of discipline, but out of a growing sense of awe and dread. Nothing had ever prepared them, mentally or emotionally, for shit like this.

Darren finally said what they had all been thinking yet too ashamed to admit to each other, "We're in a haunted fucking house. This place is evil. Can't you guys feel it? It's seen and felt the worst shit people can do. It's a fucking mean, evil, haunted crackhouse and I want to get the fuck out of here before something bad happens."

Jerry went to shut him up, but just then the group rounded the corner and found themselves in the biggest room yet. It had dark oak quarter panels around the base of the walls, and the rest was covered in moldy, decaying red wallpaper embossed with what looked like flowers. Hanging from the water-stained ceiling was the biggest goddamn chandelier that any of the guys had ever seen. Candles were burning in about half of the holders, but that gave plenty of light. There was no furniture, which was all to the good because there was no room for it; the floor was littered with eviscerated corpses.

Officer Darren, a nine-year veteran of the NYPD SWAT Team, whimpered, "Oh Christ, too late. Something bad happened."

Jerry looked over at the man who had once saved his life by shooting and killing three perps in a single firefight after taking one to the shoulder and wondered how it came to be that he now sounded like a scared little boy.

The bodies were all fresh, a fact that did little to alleviate the mounting tension amongst the men. Worse, all of the corpses had their eyes open, with faces twisted into the most god-awful expressions of terror any of the guys had ever seen, and that was saying something.

"Listen up everybody, we ain't alone here. Cover each other's backsides. No fucking ghost did this shit; I don't care what Darren says..."

"Fuck you, Dan!"

"Shut up you two," said Jerry, "and stop arguing. Pay attention to your surroundings, damn it. It don't matter what it was, the fact is we ain't alone here.

But what it was did matter to the guys. Whatever had done this had managed to do it to all of the victims at once. They only stayed in that room long enough to identify three of the corpses as Chauncy and his hired muscle. The rest looked like junkies, which only made sense. What didn't make sense was that nobody could figure out what it was that could have killed them all. Every single corpse was split open like a Thanksgiving turkey. The problem was that, upon close examination, it was clear that something had gnawed through their guts to get at the organs inside. There were teeth marks all around the tears. Big teeth marks. The kind that were normally associated with shark attacks or big game cats out of Africa. There were even teeth marks gouged into the pelvic bones of the late Mr. Winegrate.

One of the goons was missing his right arm as well, and Darren looked him over and found that his gun was gone too. The force of the bite had crushed the bone in his upper arm. Whatever this thing was, it had to have incredible strength in its jaws. Again and again, the guys were reminded of photos they had seen of shark attack victims. The catch was that no shark ever took the time to stack up their victims in nice, neat rows, or had the intelligence to bite a man's gun hand off. They faced a rational enemy. At this point, Mitch and Darren started mumbling about splitting up to find the exit from this place. All of them got the hell out of that room.

By now they realized that their watches were all working, albeit on a much slower pace. Big D. was the first to catch on that the rooms weren't exactly what they seemed either. They were carefully working their way through a set of rooms connected to a long hallway when Big D. chanced to look behind him.

"Hey guys?" he asked.

"What is it D.?" Jerry replied.

"Don't turn around O.K.?"

"All right."

"What color was the wallpaper in the hallway we just walked through?"

"A light green, I think."

"I thought so too."

Jerry turned around and saw that the wallpaper was an aqua color quite different from what he remembered. "What the...."

"Jesus and Mary, mother of God," Frankie swore. "And the carpet's different too! Look, it's brown..."

"And it used to be tan." Mitch finished.

This was too much for Darren. Something snapped inside his brain, and all of his childhood terrors and nightmares came rushing to the surface. Every boogieman, demon, and horror movie he had ever seen was in this house with him, hidden in the deep shadows all around. "Oh shit oh shit oh shit. I'm leaving man, I'm outa' here. I can't stay no longer! They're coming for us."

Jerry said, "Cut it out, man."

"We'll be next guys. I swear it!"

"Shut it, Darren, get a fucking grip!"

"We'll be next! I'm going now. If you want to live, you should run too. NOW!" With that as his exit line, Darren took off running. Mitch broke and followed right behind him. It happened so fast that they were down the dark hall and around the corner before anyone thought to give chase.

"Darren! Mitch! Stop running, stay together!" Jerry called after them.

Dan just said, "Fuck it; let's get 'em back here." and took off.

As one, the remaining three sprinted to the end of the room and turned the corner. It was a dead end. No doors or windows of any kind. Darren and Mitch had vanished.

Frankie started to giggle.

Big D. asked the question, "So what do we do now sir; find the exit, or find the guys?"

Jerry thought about it for a minute and said, "How long you think we've been in this hellhole, Dan?"

"Sir it's been at least a full day. I'm fucking exhausted, and I'm getting pretty damn hungry too."

"I figured the same thing. Right now, we need rest. I don't imagine we'll get any sleep, but an hour's rest or so might help us collect our wits and get a little energy back."

Frankie giggled and said, "Good idea sir. I'm gonna sit my ass on those stairs right behind you."

Jerry and Dan looked at each other, then turned around to follow Frankie's progress. Sure as hell, there was a fucking stairwell not twenty feet behind them. It hadn't been there before.

"What do you think sir?"

"I think that we just got really fucking lucky. What time is it Dan?"

"Glancing at his watch, he answered, "Thirty-nine seconds sir. What are you thinking?"

"Well...Fuck it. Maybe I'm as crazy as Darren, and I'll be good-damned if I can come up with a rational explanation for what's happening, but I used to love watching those weird sci-fi TV shows as a kid. What I think is this; provided there is some semblance of order to the madness here and our watches are keeping accurate time in the outside world, and provided we can find a window in one of these upstairs rooms..."

"We could find the window, bust it out, and signal the rooftop spotters."

"If our watches are keeping regular time and we're in some sort of time...uh...thing."

"So they would still be watching the windows?"

"They would be thinking that we've only been in about a half a minute. If there's any semblance of order here."

"Sir, if there isn't any sense to this we're fucked anyway."

"Well then, let's use these damn stairs before they up and disappear on us." Guns at the ready, the three men inched up the dark staircase. It felt good to be using their training to do something familiar, even if it was as dangerous as clearing an unlit stairwell. None of them really thought that they would meet any traditional bad guys waiting for them at the top, but they decided to play it by the book anyway.

Halfway up the stairs, they all stopped as a sound unlike any they had ever heard drifted to their ears. It came from upstairs and it sounded a little like the scream of a child, but it was one gut-wrenching note that seemed to contain all the pain of the world within it.

It stopped. A few seconds later it began once more.

Frankie giggled again, and Jerry saw something that just one day ago he would have bet was impossible; Big D. had tears in his eyes.

"Is that a kid?" Dan asked. "Dear God...that's a little kid. Isn't it? A little girl I think."

"Little girl, little boy – doesn't matter. It's dead." Frankie was giggling non-stop. "Come on, I'll show you!"

With that, Frankie and Dan tore up the stairs two at a time with Jerry rushing to catch up. They ran from room to room searching for the source of that sound, all pretense of safety forgotten. They shouted out to the voice. They pleaded with it. They listened to see if they were getting closer. After what must have been two or three manic hours of yelling and searching, they turned into a large room and stopped dead in their tracks.

What stopped them wasn't the fact that they were exhausted, even though they were. It wasn't that the room had a bizarre octagonal design. What stopped the three police officers cold was he fact that each wall had a doorway set into the center of it, and every doorway had been tied off--police style.

Frankie seemed to be in high spirits; he was smiling and said to the guys, "Don't give up now guys, we must have burned up what...three seconds? And hey, at least we know that the other rooms are safe--we've already cleared them!" Then he burst out into a fit of laughter that might have lasted forever if Jerry hadn't stepped forward and laid a vicious right hook to Frankie's jaw, knocking him out cold.

Dan asked, "Do you think that we've lost him, sir?"

"I don't know Dan, but let's disarm him for now and see what happens when he wakes up."

A little later Frankie was still out cold, and Dan and Jerry were resting in the room they had ended their mad chase in. The unearthly keening still came and went, but the guys were no closer to pinpointing it now than they were when they had first heard it. Dan had been withdrawn and the cries seemed to be getting to them both, so Jerry decided that he had to do something. He was no shrink, but anyone could tell that he and Dan needed each other to talk to.

"Dan."

"What's up, sir?"

"That was gonna be my question to you."

There was a moment of silence before Dan answered; the normal reticence of a man used to handling his own problems without help from anyone. Still, this was the one time in his life that Dan didn't have the answers, only doubts and concerns. Finally, he replied, "Well, I've been thinking about Frankie. I mean, he ain't the only one crackin' up in here, you know?"

"Yeah, Dan. I know."

"It's just...I really thought that it was a little girl sir; honest to God, but I should have known better than to take off like that. I do know better."

"I don't think that I can fault you, Dan. Lesser guys would have cashed it in a while ago. I'm having trouble believing we made it this far."

Dan looked at Frankie and said, "Yeah, well..."

Frankie moaned and rolled over. Jerry went over to him and knelt down by his side. Dan fingered his baton--just in case.

Frankie opened his eyes and looked around. The wailing started again. "Oh fuck, man. I was hoping this was a nightmare. Goddamn it!" He started to cry. Deep sobs escaped his throat, and his body began to shake. Jerry and Big D. were seasoned veterans, and they had dealt with their share of crap, but the sight of one of their own crying was beyond their scope.

Both of them moved off to the other side of the room to give Frankie some privacy. They sat in the shadows looking at the water-stained carpet.

Frankie cried for a long time.

Eventually, his shuddering subsided and Frankie got some control over his emotions. He wiped his eyes with the back of his hand and looked over at the other two. They were studiously watching the floor in front of their feet.

"It's all right guys; I'm back. Sorry, I put you through that, I just...Well shit, I guess I'm just not cut out for this shit. I'm sorry."

"None of us are cut out for this Frankie, but we gotta hold it together, you know? It's just us three in here. I gotta know you're back all the way; I gotta be able to trust you--Dan's' gotta be able to trust you. Can we? Are you going to freak out again? Because we're going to find the source of that noise, and we're gonna find a damn window. We're going to get the fuck out of here, but we need you tight, not giggling like a nut-job."

In response, Frankie just rubbed his jaw and said, "You got a hell of a convincing argument against that, sir."

Dan came back with, "That's not a good enough answer Frankie."

Frankie thought about that for a minute while his two brothers-in-arms waited for the truth. Finally, he told them, "I'm back, and I'll stick it out all the way."

"You back one hundred percent?"

He giggled again and answered, "No sir, eighty percent is about the best I can do."

Jerry smiled and let him off the hook, "Frankie, you at eighty percent would be thirty percent more than usual, buddy."

"Thanks a lot, sir."

Several hours later the three had explored dozens more rooms. Each time they entered a new one Frankie would call out a number signifying how many rooms they had been through. Nobody minded, even though it was freaky to hear that this small crack house contained hundreds of rooms. What bothered them was going through a previously tied-off doorway into a room that they had never been in before. Other than that, they were almost getting used to the monotony of these desiccated ruins until they entered a small dining room. It had a dingy hardwood floor, rotten striped wallpaper, and an old oblong table set for five. It also had five antique, high-backed chairs around the table. Two of the chairs around the table were occupied.

With Mitch and Darren.

They were dead of course. Even from the entranceway, it was plain to see that the bodies were in that loose-limbed posture of the freshly dead. Their eyes were open and their faces were frozen in a rictus of unbearable terror. Jerry approached them to search for a cause of death, but he already knew what he'd find--A gapping hole where his friend's guts used to be. Just like the corpses they had discovered so many hours ago downstairs, his two friends, two of the toughest guys he had ever met, had been eaten, and whatever beast had done it had put them at the dinner table.

Dan asked, bitter with resignation, "Hey sir, why do you think the table's set for five?"

Only Frankie thought it was funny. He said, "Why would it put its food in the chairs instead of on the table?"

Jerry now realized that moment was when he knew they were not getting out of this one. Not this time. The other two had come to the conclusion that Mitch and Darren had been tying off the rooms, but Jerry knew better. Darren and Mitch hadn't bothered to tie off anything. They had spent their last hours running from death. Jerry recognized his own tie-offs when he saw them. The truth was that this house didn't have any semblance of order. They were in a house of evil where the only rules were those of their unearthly tormentor. They were in a place of pain and death. That was all there was, so that was all they would find – pain and death. This Crackhouse had given birth to something horrible.

They had wandered for what seemed like forever before Big D. noticed that the crying was definitely coming from their left, and definitely getting louder. They had followed the wails for another two seconds of watch-time until they encountered another first.

"Sir? The door is closed to that room down at the end of the hallway," said Big D.

"Yeah, sir and the crying's gone too."

With a dread certainty inside, Jerry told them, "On the other side of that door we are gonna find out what killed Mitch and Darren." With less certainty, he continued, "Then we're gonna kill it. Everybody quiet; we go in hot."

With the complex hand signals they learned so long ago--back when the world was sane-- Jerry laid out the order of entry. He would go first into the hell that certainly waited to greet him and his boys on the other side. Big Dan would be second with Frankie taking up the rear and covering their ass.

Jerry squatted outside the door sweating out his fear. Nothing was routine about this job--nothing. He and his boys were New York Fucking SWAT. They never had a chance.

One thought passed through his mind; What's on the other side?

Not what's on the other side of the door. He knew what was there waiting for them all.

Death.

Rather, he wondered what came after that.

He counted down from three...

The weird, high-pitched, keening wail started from right behind the door. Something was pacing back and forth in the room.

Two...

A bright light shot out from under the door frame, illuminating the polished but well-worn boots of Jerry and Big Dan. The wailing grew louder. A clicking sound of bone upon bone penetrated the door from the other side. Jerry had a sudden vision of a gaping maw full of scythe-like teeth.

One...

Big Dan kicked in the door as Jerry swallowed his terror and dove through into the blinding light. The others were right behind him. The keening reached a fever pitch.

Zero.

# Martyr

## A Nightmare Flash Fiction

In my dreams, I'm always being crucified to the left of Christ. I've never bothered to look up or research in any way who that person may have been, or even what the symbolism might be. I don't care what my subconscious is trying to tell me. I just want the dreams to stop.

I don't care if it has anything to do with my father's ideas and practices he employed for my "Christian" upbringing. The beatings I suffered have an obvious relation to my dreams. Again, I don't care. I just want the dreams to stop, and somehow I don't think that talking out my problems at one hundred and eighty dollars an hour will help. My father died from a heart attack fifteen years ago. The dreams are much more recent. The dreams themselves are what matters.

I don't live a self-destructive life, and while I may not be the most well-adjusted person, I'm not breaking the laws of this country nor am I a threat to myself or others. Sure I find it hard to make friendships; my life as a child and young adult was hell. I'm not very trusting. How could I be? Still, the dreams only started a little while ago.

Every morning I wake up exhausted and sore. I don't need sympathy. I sure as hell don't want a priest – that you *can* blame on my father – and I don't need the stares and whispers I get when I try to explain what's happening to me. All I fucking need is a good night's sleep! Without dreams!

Maybe then I could begin the healing process because right now I'm just plain old sick. I hate dreaming about the spikes going through my feet and hands. In my dreams, they always tie my arms to the cross with ropes and put the spikes through my hands. They never stick anything in my side; they save that for Christ.

I hate the vivid realness of the dream. I hate that Christ never even looks my way. I hate the way that the Roman soldiers don't even care enough about me to taunt me as they do Jesus. I really hate the way I have to gasp for air as I slowly asphyxiate, waking just before I die.

Do you know what I hate the most, though? All the fucking blood on my bed.

# My Resignation

## Inspired by my first teaching position

The school is housed in the west wing of the hospital in what used to be the geriatric ward. Several years ago, the federal money stopped coming in for that particular age group. The new order of the day was to save the children, so the Mental Health hospital I work at went to where the money was. Out with the old, and in with the money.

The state then decreed that all children, regardless of circumstances, deserved an education. That in and of itself would have meant less than nothing to Gerald Homes Private Hospital, but the state's willingness to pay close to fifty thousand dollars a year for that education made old Dr. Gerald sit up and take notice. Fifty grand per student just to throw them in a classroom for six hours a day? How could a man like him resist?

This is where I come in. I was hired to teach math and science courses to the children here. The ages of the students here range from twelve to seventeen, but the average grade level is fourth grade. My children are not stupid, they are what we politely call "at risk" children, or E.D. – emotionally disturbed.

I deal with all the children who can't go to regular schools because of their behavior problems. Take the seven worst kids in any one school and put them into one classroom together and you get the gist of it. The hospital has all sorts of ways to classify these children and their problems. E.D. children never, ever have just one problem. They have ADHD, they have bipolar disorder, they self-medicate with alcohol or narcotics, they have true schizophrenia or multiple personality disorders, and many experience flashbacks so severe they resemble seizures.

Today is probably my last day. I just spent the last hour talking down a fourteen-year-old girl named Janice who somehow managed to get a three-foot piece of window trim pried off the big window in the main living area. She was trying to stab her roommate with it.

In the school, we classify them in three ways: bent, broken, and lifers. We don't mean it as a joke, and it certainly isn't funny, but that's how we divide them up in our heads.

The bent children like Janice don't know what love is. They've never seen it, though they desperately search. They look for love and find only pain and abuse. Their parents are never around, they live in bad neighborhoods or hang out with the wrong people. They are sexually active before they are in their teens, and they run away all the time. They are addicts. This is the child who cuts herself just to feel the pain. Caring is never real to them. The question in their mind is always; what do you really want from me?

The hospital and the school can make a genuine difference in their life, provided they don't get eaten alive by the broken ones or the lifers. They usually respond well to the personal attention and real caring shown to them by the nurses and teachers, but these kids can smell bullshit from a mile away. If the doctor, nurse, or teacher is just patronizing them, they know it and resent it. They've had enough of that on the outside; they don't need it here.

What set Janice off was that her roommate teased her about a poem she wrote for English class. It was actually a good poem.

As a teacher, I have to make sure that I am never alone with a bent student, male or female. As they grow to identify me as an authority figure, they will many times act out inappropriately. More than once I have been offered sexual favors from students barely in their teens. Spurning their advances can be tricky because if they get too angry they might accuse me of rape. We teachers look after each other and try to make sure that we are never cornered by a student alone.

Unfortunately, we can't always be there for each other, so the best we can do is to have a policy of absolute openness. When a student approaches one of us, we tell the school administration immediately and write up an incident report. Documentation will save your ass. You can't blame the children though, because for many of them, this is the first time they have had caring and stern father and mother figures in their lives.

School for them has never really been a part of their life because no one ever made them go. They are capable of learning but are embarrassed by their lack of knowledge. They don't read very well, but they catch on quickly and respond to positive feedback. However, on bad days they are the worst; they know how to disrupt and ruin a class in seconds.

But if you can reach them? Oh man, you can get by on the high of that success for weeks, maybe even months. You take the little victories wherever you can, and use them to keep going in the face of all the failure.

Now the broken ones and the lifers have a lot in common. They both come from a life that knows only hatred and evil. Not the evil spouted from the pulpit to scare up a few more dollars in the donation basket on Sunday. I mean Evil. The only real difference between the two groups is how long they lived that kind of life before the state stepped in and took them away.

Janice's roommate Charisse is broken. That means Janice is in for a world of hurt. Maybe not today, or even this week, but eventually. I know it. The therapists know it. Even the doctors know it, but there's nothing that can stop it short of sending one of the kids away forever. Human nature ensures that at some point, Charisse is going to get her chance, and she's going to take it. Charisse stabbed her brother 7 times with a butter knife to get sent here.

The children like Charisse are the ones that know about true horror. They have seen the beast at its worst; disguised as parents, relatives, neighbors, or even siblings. They know that evil exists as an actual, real live person that can invade your life at any time--day or (god forbid) night. Their stories would keep Stephen King awake.

Trust is simply another word that many of them can't spell. It isn't part of their life at all.

Their whole life has been about abuse and pain. Then, just when it can't get any worse, these children become wards of the state, to be shuffled around every few months from one Residential Treatment Center to another. Sometimes they wind up here at Gerald Homes, and sometimes they appear in my class. My job is to teach them enough to survive in the outside world. It's very unlikely that they will get placed with a foster family, so most likely they will be sent out into the world at eighteen to fend for themselves.

I try to show them enough math to be able to balance a checkbook, or at least know how to use a calculator. They won't learn anything else because it isn't relevant to them. Algebra (hah!) has nothing to do with a life that centers around being able to sleep at night without nightmares about Mommy's boyfriends visiting. Life Science doesn't impact a child who won't feel safe until he kills his mother. How do you engage a child in a class discussion about evolution when, in order to feel safe, she used a hatchet to cut the hand off of her uncle while he slept? I teach them whatever they are curious about, and try to tie it in with what they are not. In the end, though, they only learn things that they want to.

The broken ones will never be normal; they will need help and therapy for the rest of their lives. They will never be able to trust, and a part of them will forever be a little boy or girl who lived with a demon they called family. They will live a sort of half-life, always fearing the pain, but expecting it nonetheless. The state may have saved them from a life of excruciating misery, but it's at a price that many of them can't pay. Suicide lurks behind every disappointment and every setback they will experience for the rest of their lives. Charisse may commit suicide one day, but I have a real fear that she's going to take a few people with her when she does.

But at least Charisse isn't a Lifer.

Lifers. The world weeps.

We did not get to these children in time. We failed them. Utterly. They will never function in society ever. They are here because if they weren't, they would be an immediate danger to themselves and others. These children could become the serial killers of tomorrow. This is the type of child who creates a prayer book full of handwritten praise to Osama Bin Laden. They no longer fear the evil, they have grown to expect it as part of life. Some even miss it. You can never turn your back on one of these students in class.

Never.

Not if you want to go home in one piece.

We medicate these children ostensibly to help them survive. In reality, we don't know what these drugs are doing to them. There are never tests done to determine potential long-term effects on children. There are many drugs being used today that are so new that doctors don't know how they work, they just know that they seem to do the job. About half of the children respond well to their meds, and it's one of our rare victories when we see the dramatic improvements in that child in school.

The problem is that the other half seem to get worse, and the doctor's answer to that is to up the dosage. I have seen doctors prescribe medicines to a twelve-year-old in dosages large enough to medicate livestock. I've seen a fifteen-year-old go to the hospital because his liver was failing. I've seen children so spaced out that they would rather refuse their meds and face nightmares and flashbacks than feel the way they do on medication.

Somehow, I'm supposed to teach them.

There is a child in the school who has been at Gerald Homes for four years. This is an amazingly long time for a child to stay at any one place in the "system", but this is an unusual child even by our standards. To talk to the boy, you would never suspect his severe psychosis. He seems to be a rather normal, if slightly under-educated, seventeen-year-old boy capable of having a typical seventeen-year-old's life. This is until you've had a conversation with him.

This child will very calmly, and with no hint of remorse, explain to any who will listen that he did nothing wrong when he buried his two baby sisters alive in the backyard when he was thirteen years old. He knew that he would be put into a facility like this for doing it, and that's what he wanted.

It seems that the courts, for whatever reason, were unwilling to remove him from his parents' custody despite the fact that the parents were obviously doing the most vile and despicable things to him.

Then the baby girls came. Twins. And one day the boy went into the nursery and saw the video cameras and he knew what that meant.

So he took the babies out back, dug a hole, and placed them in it side by side. Then he filled the hole and went for a walk.

He went down the street to the corner and waited for an adult. When one walked by, he asked the woman to call the police because he was lost. She did so, and when the policeman arrived, my student proceeded to tell the officer the whole story. He was taken to Gerald Homes that night.

The parents are still living in the house. It isn't illegal to own video tape recorders, and though the recorders were exactly where the boy said they would be, the officers found no tapes in them or in the house.

In my students' own eyes, he did a heroic thing. He saved his twin sisters from ever having to live the life he had. It grows increasingly harder for me to disagree with him. He is required by law to be discharged out of our care and into the world in less than five months – the day he turns 18. His stated goal in life is to save others. I lie awake at night wondering what that will look like.

I've been holding this piece of broken window trim for ten minutes and thinking about this young man who killed his sisters to protect them when the news reaches me that Dr. Gerald has prescribed a fifth medication for Janice. It's a strong sedative.

It's a death sentence.

Charisse will eat her alive tonight and Janice will never even wake up. Dr. Gerald's office is directly across from the padded "time out" room that Janice is currently in. I glance over at her and I swear I see her smile at me. As if she's inside my head and can tell that I am standing in impotent rage on her behalf.

I'm looking at this piece of trim in my hand and I've decided to tender my resignation to Dr. Gerald personally. It's made of oak, I think. I swing it gently, getting the feel of the weight and balance. Maybe I can teach him something before I go.

# Tests and Results

## We create the very monsters that will destroy us.

I was never afraid of tests. That was before I knew the secret the testers were trying to hide from me. I know now that there is a foul unity of purpose at work. I know their terrifying master plan. I know that these tests are to determine if they can use me. They want to know if I'm one of them. But I'm not. I'm just a thirteen-year-old child.

Out there they called me all sorts of things. People used words like genius, strange, emotionally disturbed, and in the end, psychotic. I know what these words mean. I've read the dictionary. What terrifies me is not that they have given me these labels. What causes me to lie awake all night is why.

Once, when I was bad, Father had to lock me in a closet for three days. A Webster's dictionary was sitting on the shelf. I read by using the light sneaking through the small crack between the door and the hardwood floor. I liked the way the dictionary was laid out, very straightforward, with no gray areas. I wanted to read more books like that, so when Mother let me out I went to the encyclopedia. I read Encyclopedia Britannica from A to

Z, all 32 volumes. It took me two weeks without sleep because i could only read at night when Father was resting. I had never gone that long without sleep before. Now I don't sleep at all unless they drug me, which doesn't happen often because I'm smarter than Doctor Stephanie is. I know how to fool her.

At first, I read the Encyclopedia because it was just plain fascinating. I stayed alone in my room, only venturing out for food at breakfast time. Father and Mother never bothered with me when I stayed good. Keeping myself away from them was the best way for me to avoid doing one of the bad things or breaking one of Father's rules. Father cared deeply for the rules. It could take weeks to heal after breaking one. Sneaking out to the kitchen at night was against the rules too, so I only ate when they let me. That was usually at breakfast.

I read each volume with the dictionary by my side to look up any words I'd never seen before. Around the ninth day, I saw a pattern emerging from the Encyclopedia. In every entry, there was a poorly written paragraph that had at least four words over three syllables long. I love looking for things like that. If only I had known what was really happening!

The sentence structure in these paragraphs was stilted, as if the editor arranged the sentences around the multisyllabic words, rather than the other way around. It seemed to me that simpler words, or even the actual definition of the words in question, would have been better.

After a while, I decided to rewrite one of the paragraphs substituting the definitions for the actual words. When I had finished, I sat back and read the result. My God it fit perfectly. No more stilted sentences! At first, I thought I had to be imagining things, but with the help of repeated tests on other paragraphs, I was soon convinced that it was real. What I discovered in the Encyclopedia had to be some sort of code, a code I couldn't yet break.

I naively thought of it as a simple test. If I had known what it would reveal, I would not have solved the puzzle.

I stole a book about codes and code-breaking from my Father's collection of World War Two books to help with my efforts. When Father came home and found the book missing, he had to punish me. He didn't want to, but he had no choice. When I woke up, my books were gone and I was in a hospital bed. This time it didn't matter, Father had actually helped. His ministrations had solidified the liquid meandering and half-formed thoughts in my mind.

Encyclopedias contained information on everything. It could answer all of your questions if you knew where to look. The night I got home from the hospital, I broke into the hallway closet and got my books back.

This code I had discovered was meaningless unless you had a specific question you wanted answered. How stupid of me not to understand earlier! Something requiring this much effort to create had to serve a specific purpose. I wondered who could have created such a brilliant code, so I asked the Encyclopedia.

I pulled the volume with entries starting with N. I figured that if I needed to know about codes, the answer would be found within the NSA entry. I found the poorly written paragraph and replaced the words with their definitions. Now what? What was the entry trying to tell me?

I began experimenting. First, I counted all the extra letters added to that entry once I inserted the definitions in place of the words. That number looked a lot like a set of coordinates. The W.W.II codebook explained that some codes like this would redirect the reader to a different entry or message where the real information would be contained. Maybe these numbers were telling me what Encyclopedia volume to look in. I tried turning to the page number that corresponded. It didn't work. I toyed with the code for hours. Finally, with the first rays of sunlight coming through my window, I got an idea. I counted every word in the entry, which gave me the number 13504. I pulled out the thirteenth volume and went to flip to page 504. It only had 489. I was crestfallen.

I stared emptily at the books all around my room, and I realized that the Parents would be waking up soon. I was breaking several of Father's rules. I was going to be Punished badly. My gaze rested on a small stack of Encyclopedias by the door. They were volumes one through five, A through Er. Like a bomb going off inside my skull, I looked back down at my number 13504. Could it be? Page number and then volume? I scrambled for the book and tore it open to page 135. There staring out at me was a portrait of Leonardo DaVinci. I read the entry very carefully, and I had my answer. The code was written a long time ago by someone almost as brilliant as me. He protected the code by hiding it within itself; an incredible test. Basically, anyone not smart enough to break the code would not even know it existed. DaVinci. It fit.

I had to know more and make sure I had this code completely figured out. I asked the Encyclopedia another question. The wrong question. I asked about prodigies and their families. I felt a great fear, a sense of foreboding, settle on me as I was told that my parents were not really human. It told me that I wasn't different--they were. They were oak trees. The encyclopedia said that their roots would crush me if I let them. Oaks cared more about their roots than their acorns. Acorns are potential trees, rivals for sunlight. I didn't want to believe the books, but I had no choice. I already knew the code was telling the truth. Heart thumping in my chest, I read on.

The encyclopedia showed me how to get rid of them. It said that I had to do it immediately, before sunrise, or they would steal my sunlight forever. I set about at once, limbs shaking with the knowledge that the world would assume I had killed two people; the two people who gave me life. It was a gruesome task the Encyclopedia had set for me, but it worked perfectly. As I stood, chest heaving, bloody, and spattered with gore, I felt a great sense of relief to know once and for all that the code was The Truth.

The police questioned me of course, and they were pretty sure that I had done it, but the encyclopedia guided my actions and they could do nothing but send me to special doctors. The doctors came with dozens of tests.

I knew that I had to pass these tests or face dire consequences. What those consequences were, I couldn't fathom. I supposed, however, that death was the least of my worries.

Most of the tests were easy at first. Then they got frustrated at me because I knew so much and they couldn't fail me, so they started giving oral exams with questions that didn't have answers.

They would ask me evil, cruel questions like, "Your parents were killed with an axe, how does that make you feel?"

Another question was, "How did you feel about the way your Father treated you?"

I got confused when they asked me these questions. It took me such a long time to look the answers up in the appropriate Encyclopedia, and the answers were always so vague that it was hardly worth the effort. The doctors didn't want me to use the Encyclopedia or the Webster's Dictionary. By the time they thought to take the Dictionary from me, it was too late; I had it memorized. When they took the Encyclopedias I sat there quiet, unmoving, until one day an angry psychologist told me, with a smirk on his face, that the answer couldn't be found in the encyclopedia. Nevertheless, the volumes were returned to me. I relaxed. If they were not smart enough to know the truth then I could certainly pass their tests.

\*\*\*

They tell me here that my IQ is 187, but I think that they lie. 187 does not begin to cover it. It's not an intentional lie though, I can always tell by their facial expressions and body language when they do that. No, they're lying to themselves; they don't want to believe that a thirteen-year-old boy can be as smart as I am. Their tests can't measure my intelligence and they know it. I'm a danger to them, and one day they will murder me if I can't destroy them first. I can see the same fear in their eyes that Father had.

\*\*\*

The doctors and nurses say that they want to help me. The encyclopedia says that is true, but it also told me that they really want to help me become one of them. It told me what they are, and it told me what I have to do to protect myself.

They have held me here for six months. I've got the Encyclopedia memorized A through V. I can do the computations entirely in my head now, and every day I get faster. I've been going to a special school at the hospital, just for the children's patients. My teachers think I'm very smart. I have yet to get a single wrong answer on a test. The encyclopedia guides me. I just tell them that I read a lot.

My teachers say that I'm very efficient and that this is a good thing, an important thing. I knew that they would think so, given their true, nightmare nature.

The nurses here, the doctors, orderlies, even the teachers; they aren't human. They're ants. It makes my skin crawl to be near these insects in human skin. It would be a blessing if I wasn't the only one to know, but they would kill any of the real humans here who found out about them. I dare not tell anyone, this is my burden to bear. The Encyclopedia tells me all of this and more.

Ants live in nests, like this hospital. Their organization is a model of efficiency, like this hospital. Ants have highly evolved social structures;

each part of the nest specialized, children's ward, adult ward, school, and administration. Each group of ants specialized for their task, doctors, orderlies, teachers, secretaries.

It took me a long time to finally learn what these things have in store for me. They want me to be a teacher ant. They want me to teach others the code. They keep asking me how I do the things I do and how I know the things I know. They want me to give away what I've so dearly paid for.

I understand now why Da Vinci had to hide this mystical code. The truth is strange and terrible beyond anything I could have imagined. I have heeded his advice, and so am now writing my notes in a code of my own invention.

\*\*\*

I know that the real reason they keep me separated from the other kids isn't because I'm so much smarter than them, even though that's what the principal says. The real reason is that those kids are real kids, humans, most of them anyway. The ants work to keep them crazy and unbalanced. The encyclopedia told me that their medications alter perceptions for the worse, not for the betterment of patients, as claimed. That way, they can be controlled by the ants, and programmed to serve them, like worker drones. They don't want me for anything like that, so I can't be around anything like that. I could pick up bad habits.

They secretly tell the other kids that I'm too dangerous to take classes with them, but that's just not true as long as they're really human. A kid on my floor, Greg, is a viper. One day after he pushed me down in the hall and started to kick me, he yelled that I was a psycho freak just because the doctors had me in leather shackle restraints. The doctor's excuse was, of course, that I was a danger to myself and others, so the courts ordered the restraints be worn at all times. They knew I was smart enough to escape from their nest otherwise. I asked the encyclopedia why Greg did this to me, and the books told me that Greg was a snake. A viper to be precise, and that his poison could kill me. I looked up how to kill snakes. Their whole body is one long neck. Some people hunt snakes. Snake hunters will grab a snake by its head and crack the snake like a whip. Snap the neck; kill the snake. If there is a next time with Greg, it will end differently. I have to protect myself. I owe it to humanity.

Da Vinci knew how dangerous this code would be in the wrong hands. The truth is a powerful weapon against creatures such as these, who have good reason to fear it. Out there in the free world, we humans still out-number these abominations. They are not ready to enslave us yet. We could still win the war, but in here it's just me and a bunch of crazy people. I can count on no one but my Encyclopedia and me.

\*\*\*

I have to burn this nest down soon. Almost everything is in place now; I'm just waiting for the right moment. When you burn out an ant nest, you have to make sure that the queen ant is killed, or the nest will just be rebuilt. The queen ant here is Dr. Gerald. It wasn't hard to figure out, the place is named after him. I'm sure that he is the queen, even though he's not female. I know the books are never wrong.

The problem is that I have not seen Dr. Gerald for many days. They say he's been interviewing for several open positions and having meetings, but the books say that he is getting ready to breed new ants. Why do they think they can fool me?

This hive is very old; the heaters in the school area are gas. I can never get to the gas lines in school because the teacher ants are very watchful, mistrusting creatures. They've seen a lot of childish attempts at vandalism during their time here. What they do allow me is use of the computer. They have a computer lab in the school just for the students. Only one is hooked up to the Internet, and most kids are forbidden to use it. That one is really for the teachers to use, but they give me special privileges because of my potential usefulness to them. I've been surfing educational and Vo Tech sites.

They even let me take a computer disk back to my ward for homework. We have one very old computer in the common room. Most of the kids use it to play video games. I'm not supposed to carry the computer disk, but I've been whining at the nursing assistant who walks me back and forth from school to the children's ward. I keep telling her she doesn't know how to load it, use it, or even carry it properly. One day about two weeks ago, she threw it at me and said that I could just do it all myself then without any help from her at all. I think she meant it as punishment. Now I carry it by myself every day. Last night, she forgot to ask for it back. That gave me time to finish the virus.

\*\*\*

Today could be the day. My teachers say that they are giving me the SAT. They tell me that it is the most important test I'll ever take. The Encyclopedia agrees that I'll be tested like never before, and that can mean only one thing; they are going to try and convert me. I don't know how they'll do it, what terrible process they will use, but I won't let them turn me against humanity. I don't know if I can do this, but I have to try. I am the best mind humanity has, and I can't let them down. I have never been afraid of tests before.

Doctors and teachers have been in and out of my schoolroom all week, and my notes have been removed while I was at school. Thankfully, they have not discovered the hiding spot behind my dresser drawer. Inside is a battery I stole from the TV remote control in the common room. Next to it is some of the steel wool lifted from the cafeteria, and a thin metal rod from my dresser drawer.

They are coming for me in about five minutes to take me to the computer room. I'll have everything ready for the test. All of my secret tools will go with me. If Dr. Gerald is there, or if they leave me no choice, I'll burn this nest down. I don't think that I'll make it out alive, but there is a chance I might.

***

The nest has been severely damaged. My plan worked almost perfectly, but I can not understand why the Encyclopedia didn't warn me about Greg. The snake has cost me dearly. Now, they think that it is over. The Ants think that I have failed and that they have won. Nothing could be farther from the truth.

My Encyclopedia helped me form the last plan, and it is helping me with the new one. It has told me that I really need to review my past mistakes and pay closer attention to what it says. Now that I am forced to go entirely from memory, I must take extra pains to ensure that I do not miss a thing or leave something out of my computations. I can do it. I have to. My job is not yet finished.

When the Teacher Ants took me to the computer lab to start the SAT's, I went straight to the main computer as if I didn't realize that the test would be written on paper. The Teachers were so busy getting a table cleared for me that I had time to put in my virus. It attacked the mainframe, just like the Encyclopedia said it would.

Their terror began shortly thereafter. Code yellow alarms began sounding in all the treatment units almost simultaneously, so the orderlies followed protocol and rushed back to their respective units to help contain the patients. I continued to work as if nothing unusual was occurring and even pulled up my lesson plans from school. The teachers actually stopped working to discuss what was happening. Only a few minutes later, the fire alarms went off and the lights all over the hospital, along with everything else electrical, shut down.

Because the computer room is at the center of the building and has no windows, the room was cast into total darkness. In the confusion, I was able to pry the gas line going into the heating unit free from its housing by using the metal bar from a dresser drawer. What I did next I learned from an educational website. The irony of that pleased me. I had learned that sending an electrical charge through steel wool can cause it to ignite. I used the smuggled battery and steel wool to accomplish just that. It took a couple of seconds longer than I thought it would, and my already racing heart beat even faster. I was sure that the Teachers would get me before I could get my homemade flame-thrower working.

I felt a pair of hands grab me just as the steel wool smoldered and burst into flames. I coupled it with the gas line and turned it on the teacher holding me first. The fire singed my hair and eyebrows, but the Ant caught fire, and she ran screaming from the room wreathed in flames. I turned it upon the other Teacher, as he stood wide-eyed with horror at what had just happened to its colleague. Both were engulfed and ran through the school spreading the fire wherever they went bumping into things.

At this point, I could have run away. My planning was thorough enough, even unto creating a virus that would shut down all of the safety features like magnetic doors. However, I would not take advantage of the opportunity to escape them yet. I had a responsibility. Instead, I would use this chance to kill as many Ants as possible. I needed to make sure that the nest was destroyed.

I ran to another classroom on the other side of the unit and repeated the process of flame-thrower creation. The entire east wing was ablaze within fifteen minutes. Most of the Ants were running for the exits to escape the flames, and nobody was paying much attention to the patients, so I was able to go out the doors and hobble to the west wing. There I would have continued to wreak havoc, If not for that viper Greg.

Children and other patients were everywhere and there just wasn't enough staff to control them all, so I was able to travel down the hallways unmolested. As I turned the corner, I ran headlong into Greg going the other way. He recoiled from the impact appearing as if he was just going to go around me, but I saw the truth. He was getting ready to strike. He was going to use the opportunity that I had created to kill me! What the viper did not know was that I was ready for it. I stepped to the side, just as the Encyclopedia told me to, and as the viper went by me I grabbed it by the neck and twisted violently to the side. I heard the reassuring crunch of broken bone, and I let the snake fall to the floor.

It was oddly stilled in death. I had expected it to writhe around in its final throes of agony, and I waited to see if Greg's body would move at all. That was my fatal error.

A Worker Ant had chanced to glance up this hallway as it ran by and saw what I did. These orderlies may not have cared about the patients running for their lives, but they certainly cared about me killing one of their allies. I had not realized that the Vipers worked with the Ants until that very moment when a pair of large, callused hands closed on my arms and I was thrown to the ground with a force that knocked the wind from my lungs. Before I could get my breath back, two hundred and forty pounds of disgusting alien Ant dropped on my back, and I heard the creature call to more of its kind to help restrain me.

I was helpless under that orderly, and there, in the middle of an inferno, the Ants stuffed me into a full body restraint they called "The Bag". Then they left me there to die in the encroaching flames of my own creation.

Somchow, the flames were brought under control around the same time that the nurses and orderlies returned to the hallway where I lay. I was carried to this isolation room where I remain still. The story was not long in being pieced together, and my role in the conflagration was revealed.

I am not allowed any freedom of movement anymore, nor can I have any interaction with other patients. The ants have figured out that I know their secret. They are trying to decide what to do with me. The Encyclopedia in my head tells me all of this. I don't even have to use the code anymore. The entries have sorted themselves out in my mind, and now I have access to any answer I need. It talks to me.

Right now I'm waiting for an answer on how to escape from this room. It will come. The Encyclopedia will never let me down. I'll pass the test. I'll get the answer.

It will come.

# Hookers From Outer Space

## Terror from out there

"Why-oh-why do they always try to look like a hooker?"

"Well, I think it has something to do with the unique opportunities regarding that ahh... profession as it were."

"Jack?"

"Yeah, Malachy?"

"Shut the fuck up."

Jack shut his mouth and seemed to shrink down into his upturned coat collar. He idly wondered why his partner asked him questions if he didn't want the answers. He stared at the remains of their latest hunt. The only thing left of the alien creature was a singed leg sporting a crisscrossing pattern of dark lines. It was lying in the light snowfall blanketing the streets of Paris, France. It had been wearing fishnet pantyhose. Dressed like a hooker from the 1980's or something. Sickened, Jack turned to his partner for perhaps the thousandth time in the six months they'd been hunting together, and he tried again to figure Malachy out.

Malachy O'Brian was a larger-than-life legend out here on the fringes. Stories of his unique brand of hunting had even made it as far as Africa. Jack couldn't figure out why. Malachy was about a foot shorter than everybody, with a scrawny little body that could only be described as wiry by a sympathetic friend. Yet Malachy was feared by every Alien type in Europe.

Most hunters picked an area and just started hunting. Not Malachy. He roamed the continent, hunting for a few days or weeks before suddenly packing up and traveling perhaps a thousand miles to the next country and city, only to hunt there for a while, and then do it all again.

There were three distinct "species" of aliens, and all three had to deal with hunters like Malachy and Jack. For the most part, that meant killing the hunters just like anybody else. The average career of a hunter lasted about two and a half years, and Jack was well aware that he was pushing the statistical limit. It took a certain type of man to commit suicide in this way, but the world always seemed to have plenty in reserve. For his part, Jack was beginning to have thoughts of quitting, though no hunter ever did.

Malachy had been at it for thirteen years. Thirteen! Almost since the beginning.

Jack had seen a picture of Malachy taken right after he had started this insane career. As far as he could tell, in thirteen years Malachy's hair had gone mostly gray, and his face had a few more lines in it, but that was it. He hadn't gained a pound or lost a step, but somehow Jack doubted that the Malachy of thirteen years ago had been this tired.

Thirteen years. Shit, the Aliens only showed up seventeen years ago. One day; life as usual. The next? The next day teachers were ripping their students limb from limb, preachers were devouring their parishioners when they went into the confessional, and johns were literally getting eaten alive by hookers. Later investigation would reveal that overnight, throughout the world, people who came into contact with large numbers of other human beings on a regular basis had been mutilated and consumed in their homes the night before, and for some reason, their skins were the only thing left behind.

Of course, things went nuts after that. Religious freaks proclaimed that the end was nigh, but don't they always? Most of the world religions refused comment or issued a statement that they were praying for the world. Only the Catholic Church, in the form of the Pope, had anything important to say. The Pope went on air across the world to tell his flock that these were most certainly not Demons or minions of hell and that it was foolish to think so. He went on to say that such thinking was medieval and showed only an ignorance of the scriptures to believe any such thing. Privately, however, the Pope had a few interesting "thoughts" on what might be effective against these terrors.

China went and nuked Taiwan, the Korea's destroyed each other, and nobody cared. The United Nations disappeared as an entity in less than twenty-four hours. It was every nation for itself. India took the opportunity to invade Cashmere and found it totally populated with Aliens. Their military force was decimated. The exact same thing happened to the Israelis. They immediately blamed the Palestinians and sent in their forces. Very few made it back. However, the world did learn that these things could be killed. It just took serious firepower. Later, the leaders of the world would point to these two examples of how incredibly prepared these aliens were, and how much knowledge about world affairs they must have had, as a way of exonerating themselves from any perceived blame.

For about ten seconds in America, the Feds feared that hundreds, if not thousands of their citizens would be joining up with all those pesky survivalist groups. Then the word came down the pipe; They were all dead. Every single one from every single group.

The immensity of all of these the attacks stunned the entire world into momentary inaction. The reports kept coming in: Russia, Canada, Japan, Africa, and even Australia. Nowhere was safe. The entire Earth was under attack.

One week later, it stopped as suddenly as it had begun. The Aliens hunkered down, and the ravaging of planet Earth settled into a routine. Many people held the view that it was because communities had banded together to provide protection for each other. Those running what survived of the world governments knew better. Military men: Generals, Admirals, Marshals, and Warlords alike had banded together by radio and worked as a worldwide unit. Many times, against orders, they experimented with troops lent to each other as the need arose, to find out how best to kill the damn enemy. Turned out that together we had the advantage in firepower. These aliens could eat up bullets to the body and keep coming until you literally shot off their legs, but it also became obvious that they burned like torches if you could set them on fire.

Once we started fire bombing any place they grouped up and to hell with the collateral damage, the creatures split up and went their own ways. Now we had to track them down and kill them one at a time.

Rank and file soldiers weren't cut out for that kind of action (though they most certainly tried), and special forces units didn't have nearly enough men to cover their own countries, let alone the world. The call went out through every corner of the earth--If you want to save what's left of this world, we need volunteers. We need hunters.

Those who had lost loved ones, seen family butchered, or been forced to watch as their world fell apart volunteered in droves those first few years. It was revenge they were after. What they got, more often than not, was dead. The aliens were faster, meaner, and stronger than humans. And they were not beasts, though they killed and ate humans in a frenzy of violence. No, they were smart.

The average hunter had a shotgun with incendiary rounds supplied by the militaries of the world. That's it.

"Hey, Malachy?"

"Yeah?" he sighed out.

"Why the hell are you still doing this?"

"It needs to be done."

"Bullshit."

Malachy sighed, "Jack, what did I tell you the day we teamed up?"

Jack looked down at the ground frustrated, "Don't ask you questions."

"About?"

"About anything."

Malachy held up his hands and shrugged, "So what are we doing here?"

"God damn it, Malachy, we've been killing these monsters together for half a year and I know less about you than I know about them! And I don't know shit about them!"

"You know plenty. I've taught you. You can identify the three different types even when they are disguised as humans now. That's hard to do."

"I'm not talking about the aliens. I'm talking about you, don't change the subject."

"I hate them, Jack. Okay? I'm not special, there's no interesting story. I hate them for the same reason we all do. They ate my family."

"Come on Malachy. You've survived about ten years longer than any other hunter anyone has ever heard of. There's something to that."

"Yeah. I'm still too angry to die. One of these bastards will get me eventually, Jack. But so far I'm still so damn pissed off when I fight one, I'm just not willing to quit until the thing is burned to a crisp."

"Malachy, my wife and daughter died when one of these things got into our house three years ago. I've been hunting ever since. But I'm tired of it. I've had my revenge and it's fixing nothing."

Malachy cursed and spat on the ground, "Then get the hell away from me before you get us both killed. I haven't had my revenge yet, the one who wronged me is still out there."

Jack was astonished at the revelation, "You're hunting a specific alien? How? Why? What the hell?"

"You know the legends of the fourth alien?"

"Sure, everybody has heard the tales. A mythical fourth type that is some sort of 'leader' or overlord. It's bullshit."

Malachy stared at Jack, "It's very, very real. And I'm at war with it."

Jack sputtered and finally repeated himself, "How?"

"Like I said, the damn thing ate my family. It should have eaten me too, but it decided to taunt me first. It played with me. Toyed with me the whole time it ate my children. It exists, it's been running all over Europe for the last two years, and I've been tracking it."

Jack couldn't wrap his head around it. It was just too big. "But...how? I mean, how are you alive? How are you tracking it? How do you know where it is? How, damn it!"

Malachy looked at Jack with a wry smirk, "Well, I escaped obviously. I'm tracking it by following the swarms. Wherever he goes, his...minions...I'd guess you call them, swarm human enclaves to provide him with food. It's fairly obvious if you're looking for it. And that's how I know where he *was*. As for finding where he *is*, that's proving to be the hard part."

"Are you seriously telling me that you have proof of a leadership-level alien and you haven't told anyone? What the fuck, Malachy? This could change the war! This could fucking *win* the war!"

Malachy growled, "I'm not interested in the war or the world, Jack. I'm interested in killing one fucking alien. One. When that's done, I don't care what happens to the world."

Jack just stared for a long moment. "Jesus fucking Christ, Malachy, that's cold. Even for you."

Malachy stared back at Jack. "You're right, you don't know me at all."

Jack clenched and unclenched his fists a few times before saying, "Okay. So you're hunting a 'super alien'. Why are we here killing a single hooker from outer space?"

"There was a swarm here just last week. I've never been closer. We're right behind them now."

Suddenly there was an eerie, unearthly, echoing cackle from the building behind them.

Then the voice came out of the shadows. It spoke in English from a mouth that evolved for something totally different. It slurred, hissed, and garbled the words, but Jack had no trouble understanding what it said, and it scared him to immobility.

*"Nnnuuhh. Hi aaam beehyint hue, hyuntersh."*

Malachy had no such frozen moment of fear. He spun toward the building and sent incendiary rounds through all three windows facing the street in a rapid-fire of pump action death.

Inside, the alien laughed.

Because Jack had frozen in place, he was the one who saw the other aliens begin creeping out of every doorway on the street. "Malachy!"

Malachy had been staring at the building he had fired on and was rapidly reloading the shotgun with three more rounds when he hear Jack and took a glance back, "Shit." He finished loading the gun, but then let it hang in his hand down at his side.

Jack repeated. "Malachy!"

"Stand down, Jack, we don't have the firepower to win this."

Jack whimpered, "Oh fuck."

"Be strong, man!" Malachy barked. "We might not be able to kill 'em all, but we still might live through this if you get your shit together."

"How?"

*"Yeesshh. Hyow?"* An alien unlike any Jack had seen before walked out of the burning building and stood on the sidewalk about twenty feet away. *"Ay ahm...kuriushh?"* This alien stood about six and a half feet tall and where most aliens were lean to the point of emaciation, this one was full bodied and looked more muscled.

Malachy pointed his empty hand at the alien, "By killing you, of course."

It threw it's head back and laughed that horrific laugh, *"Hyuntersh. Yurr fyire ish nah gud. Ay dunt bern. Mah shildrun weel feasht un hue."*

Through his fear, Jack could see Malachy was standing tall and calm in front of this monster. He couldn't understand it. This was the nightmare of every hunter, finding themselves surrounded by more alien's than they could kill and getting eaten alive. Yet Malachy seemed to be enjoying himself.

"Jack," he called out, "Do not fire your gun. For any reason. Understand me?"

Jack nodded, but Malachy wasn't looking at him, so he asked again, "Jack! Do you understand?"

"Yes," he whispered. Then stronger, he cleared his throat and said, "Yes."

"If you shoot that gun we are both dead. You understand?"

Giddy with fear, Jack cried out, "I said I won't shoot, Malachy, but no. No, I do not understand."

"Fair enough. Remember I said I escaped from this bastard?"

"Yeah?"

"I was able to because his soldiers won't interfere with a fight between leaders, and only leaders fight each other. When I fought this bastard the first time, they all assumed I was a leader. Then I was able to get free and run. But if you engage the soldiers, they'll treat you like food. Got it?"

Jack knew what they treated food like. A frenzy of tearing, ripping, biting, and eating. He nodded again but included, "Got it, Malachy. No shooting."

The alien was staring at them through this whole exchange with a surprisingly human expression on it's face and a classic confused head tilt.

*"Hwee haf fite onesh? Nut poshible. Hall dyie. Hue dyie. Non eshcape."*

In answer, Malachy dropped the shotgun and charged the Alien, screaming.

The alien stood shocked at the charge and began to laugh as it opened its arms and flexed its backward knees to meet Malachy's rush, but at the last instant, Malachy leapt impossibly high into the air and slammed his hands and arms around the alien's head.

The nightmare squealed in surprise as it staggered backward and reached up to grab Malachy to tear him off, but Malachy simply refused to let go as he began tearing at the alien's head, eyes, and whatever those layered flaps of skin ringing the crown of its skull were.

With a start, Jack saw that the other aliens were frozen, looking for all the world as if they had turned to stone. He turned his attention back to the fight in front of him.

The fight between Malachy and the alien was nothing but an animal frenzy of tearing, clawing, and screaming. Neither used any technique or fighting skills that Jack could see. They each tore big chunks out of each other, and the bright scarlet blood that both species – human and alien – seemed to share, splattered all around them both.

Eventually, they collapsed onto the street and the fight went to the ground, where it became a swirling and twisting contest where both fighters tried to get a headlock or a choke on the other. Jack cried out in fear as the alien spun onto Malachy's back and got a bloody arm wrapped around his face, but Malachy savagely bit into the alien's arm, tearing out a mouthful of muscle and gore, causing the alien to screech in pain and pull back, shocked at the huge chunk taken out of his arm.

Malachy spun his body around while still in the loosened grasp of the monster so that they wound up face to face, and something in Malachy's eyes must have spelled the end for the alien because the screech died out and a mewling sound came from its throat as Malachy used his mouth again to clamp down over the alien's neck and began to chew.

It was the single most disgusting thing Jack had seen in his three years of hunting, and he couldn't help but think the real beast in front of him wasn't the alien at all, it was this animal that had once been Malachy.

The other aliens began to sway in unison and a low rumble that was so deep it was almost felt by Jack rather than heard, began to emanate from the assembled beasts.

Suddenly, the other alien stopped moving and Malachy unclenched his jaw from around the alien's throat. He stood up and spat a mouthful of blood and chewy bits into the face of the alien before stepping back and looking up towards Jack. For a moment, the animal rage and lust for blood was still so strongly present on Malachy's face, that Jack involuntarily took a step back, shocked and terrified.

Malachy then shuffled over to the closest alien soldier and stared into its eyes, saying nothing.

Abruptly, the low bass rumble stopped, and the aliens all melted back into the shadows of the burned-out buildings from which they had emerged so recently.

Finally, Jack worked up the nerve, "What just happened?"

Wiping blood off his face and chin, Malachy answered, "I just avenged my family."

"Malachy...," he tried to continue but found he couldn't.

"What, Jack?"

"What the hell are you?"

Malachy sighed, "Don't ask questions, Jack. Haven't I told you that over and over again?"

"Yeah, but for fucks sake, there's no way a human can outfight an alien! They are so much faster and stronger than us. That thing should have torn you limb from limb! How did you kill it with your bare hands?"

Malachy hung his head, "God damn it, Jack, I like you. Stop asking questions."

"No! No, Malachy. You like me? Great. Then tell your friend Jack what the hell just happened!"

Malachy looked up into Jack's face and said nothing for a few seconds before sadly shaking his head and saying, "Fine. I'll tell you."

"Good."

"What I told you about my family is true. That fucker killed them and ate them. He did it to take over my kingdom. I just took it back. My hordes are going home now. The earth won't need hunters any longer. I suppose that's a good thing."

Jack just stared in growing horror as what Malachy said filtered through his amped-up brain.

"You mean...you...are an alien? Like that?" he cried, pointing to the dead alien on the ground.

Malachy sneered, "Like that? Hell no. That's a Pishach demon. A flesh eater."

Jack was lost, "A what?"

Malachy looked at Jack with a hint of sympathy, "We're not aliens, we're what you would more accurately call demons. That fucker there took my kingdom in a coup. I had three armies; Fiends, Skinwalkers, and your favorite," he pointed to the leg of the alien that had been disguised as a hooker, "Succubi. He used them to feast, like a spoiled child with a new toy."

Jack started crying, "And what are you?"

Malachy sighed as he walked over to him, and gently took his shotgun from out of his unresisting hands. "Sorry Jack, I really did like you."

Still crying, he quietly repeated, "What are you?"

"I'm hungry."

# About the author

Daniel Nick has been called many things. The ones safe to repeat in public include special education teacher, sailor, martial artist, biker (the kind with loud engines and leather jackets), world traveler, rock climber, sculptor, writer, actor, ADHD adult, husband, dog lover, and more that would probably bore you. Daniel Nick prefers to be called an artist, and maybe a good person.

In real life, he created the One World Martial Arts Federation, a fully inclusive and adapted martial arts organization for students of all abilities and embraces the honor of being the representative of the International Thiang Bando Association for the Americas.

Hey! No more third person. Hi! Join my newsletter and check out what I'm up to if you want: www.danielnick.com

And remember, there's nothing that says "Thank you" to an author like giving a review online somewhere

*Daniel Nick*

# Also by Daniel Nick

Café Muse – a short story in the Anthology, Coffee and Dreams Volume 2

Doubly Blessed – a short story in the Anthology, Coffee and Dreams Volume 3

Root of all Evil – a short story in the Anthology, Coffee and Dreams Volume 4

Seven Degrees Off Horror – A Horror Anthology

War Dog – Book One of Hound of the Gods

The Hands That Feed (coming 2026) – Book Two of Hound of the Gods

Mad Dogs (coming 2027) Book Three of Hound of the Gods

www.ingramcontent.com/pod-product-compliance
Lightning Source LLC
Chambersburg PA
CBHW050834180626
46814CB00004B/1619